DATE DUE

PREPOSTEROUS FABLES FOR UNUSUAL CHILDREN

The Tooth Fairy

The Maestro

The Sorceror's Last Words

Wolf

THE MAESTRO

Written and illustrated
by Judd Palmer

BAYEUX

Special thanks to those who contributed so enormously to the conception and realization of this book: Doug McKeag & Onalea Gilberston, Dave & Jenny Lane, Jim Palmer, and the Old Trouts: Shannon Anderson, Peter Balkwill, Bobby Hall, Steve Kenderes, and Steve Pearce.

THE MAESTRO
© 2002 Judd Palmer and Bayeux Arts, Inc.
Published by: Bayeux Arts, Inc., 119 Stratton Crescent SW, Calgary, Canada T3H 1T7 www.bayeux.com

Cover design by David Lane & Judd Palmer
Typography and book design by David Lane
Edited by Jennifer Mattern

Canadian Cataloguing-in-Publication Data
Palmer, Judd. The maestro
    ISBN 1-896209-78-5
    I. Title.
PS8581.A555M33 2002   jC813'6   C2002-910521-8
PZ7.P185535Ma 2002

First Printing: October 2002
Printed in Canada

The Publisher gratefully acknowledges the financial support of the Canada Council for the Arts, the Alberta Foundation for the Arts, and the Government of Canada through The Book Publishing Industry Development Program.

For Sophie

There once was a town beset by sorrow.

Chapter One

THERE ONCE WAS a town that was beset by sorrow. It was haunted by a misery so deep it was like a fog; it filled the cobbled streets, clogging the gutters and eavestroughs, clinging to the barren branches of the trees and to the pant-legs of people in the street. That fog never lifted. The sun could not penetrate the gloom.

The town sat on the edge of a grey

river, its buildings huddled along the banks like depressed hunchbacks made of stone. They were rain-stained and grim, those buildings, and chilly. They were ponderous and uninviting. They had shadowed doorways and dark windows and curtains that fluttered forlornly in the hollow wind.

All around the town were jagged mountains, which looked down on the streets like the frowning faces of some unsympathetic supreme court. Their faces were cold, and their foreheads wreathed in clouds. They cast a long and tattered shadow over the town like judges' robes.

In the mountains were quarries, where the townsfolk would toil. Every morning, everybody would file out of their houses with picks and shovels on their shoulders, themselves as grey as the stones they beleaguered. Stooped, grunting, old spines creaking, they shuffled to the mountains to hack away at the cliffs with their iron tools all day. And then, as the feeble sun disappeared behind the cold crags, they would form a ragged line and march, exhausted, back to their houses. Like the dwarfs of old, who, in the sunless caverns of the earth, spent their drudgerous days, the people of the town knew only the heaving muscle, the jarring scrape of their shovel blades, the sweating brow.

Such was life in the dreary town. What made it a particularly dreadful town, however, was this: There was absolutely no music in it. You'd never hear musicians on a Friday night, or a melody through a window on laundry day, or even just somebody whistling while walking down the street. Once in a while, you'd hear somebody cough or sniffle, or drop something in the kitchen. But other than that, the only sound you could hear was the insistent clang and crunch of the quarries in the distance.

But there was something else, even more horrible. Something strange; something—perhaps—evil. There were no children in that town at all. Everybody in it was altogether old. The town was empty of chatter, laughter, running, swinging, dancing, and all the other things children are fond of doing. The summer brought no screams of delight, for there was no school to let out for the holidays; the river saw no splashing or surreptitious swimming; the tree branches never felt the weight of grubby toes, and the puddles lay dank and murky, undisturbed by stomping rubber boots.

Why was the town this way? Why was it beset by such sorrows? Why did the townsfolk toil in the mountains? Why was there no music? Why were there no children? What secret sadness haunted that place? We shall find out. For now, all we know is that nobody in their right minds would ever want to move there.

Alas! Somebody did move there. She is the hero of our story.

Her name was Hannah, and she was a young girl. The

reason she moved there is very sad: In those days, doctors had not found the cures to many illnesses, which we now have no reason to fear. But Hannah's parents had been stricken by consumption, and died shortly after, leaving her an orphan. Her only relatives lived in the town we have been discussing, so she was sent to live with them. She had no choice.

Hannah came to the town to live with her aunt and uncle, Greta and Otto Groebelfälter. They were not pleased to take Hannah in. They had no children of their own, of course, and they had no idea what to do with little Hannah. They much preferred to absorb themselves in their work in the mountains. But they had no choice but to take the girl. They resigned themselves to the task of parenthood, and told her everything she needed to know about her new life on the day she arrived: "No music," they said. "Only rock-smashing."

There could be no worse place in the world for Hannah to have ended up—this town, where they hated music. Hannah loved music more than anything. She would spend all her time, when she should have been learning about rock-smashing, dreaming about music.

"Time for your homework," Aunt Greta said.

Chapter Two

IN HER MIND, it was a symphony. There was a concert hall inside her head. The ceiling was a vast dark dome, and there was a grand entranceway—her teeth were a beautiful pearl staircase, and her tongue was a red carpet for all the important people who came to hear. Her eyes were stained glass windows which cast a shimmering gleam on the orchestra where her brain should be. And she herself was the *prima donna*, the lead singer, standing in front of all the musicians, and her voice was high and powerful, filling her skull with a melody that poured out of her ears and nose so that the whole world stopped in its tracks to listen.

"Hannah? Hannah? Where are you, Hannah? It's time for you to do your homework. Where is that strange girl?"

Right in the middle of her favourite part, the part where she sang the high note, and all the people in her head rose to their feet and applauded madly, somebody threw open the doors and interrupted. Blinding light streamed into the concert hall, the audience turned blinking to see who could be so rude as to be shouting at the *prima donna* in the middle of her aria.

It was her Auntie Greta. Hannah's dream collapsed in on itself. The orchestra ran in terror, the audience scrambled to look for their coats.

"What were you doing? Daydreaming again?" grunted her aunt.

"Yes Auntie, I'm sorry," said Hannah.

Aunt Greta frowned, which is to say her face changed not at all from its normal expression. She stood with her enormous arms crossed across her chest, covered as usual with rock-dust from her work at the quarry. She was so coated in it that she had the appearance of a ghost; her eyebrows were thick with grey, her tight bonnet (where it stuck out from her dirty kerchief) was stiff with it. The hair on her muscled arms was hoary with grime.

Hannah was hiding in the closet. In amongst the coveralls and trench-coats and rubber boots, she thought she might stay hidden long enough from her aunt to get to the high-note part of the symphony, but unfortunately Aunt Greta's determination to keep Hannah in line was invincible. Especially when it was time for homework.

"Time for your homework," Aunt Greta said, producing a small boulder from behind her back.

Hannah crept out of her hiding place and regarded the rock with a great sadness. It was all that awaited her here in this dreadful town. Her future was hard and cold and grey, just like her aunt, just like this stone, just like the whole town. But Hannah was soft and warm and colourful, like the music in her head, the music she remembered from when her parents were alive.

Greta was not unkind; she wanted Hannah to understand, and was a fine teacher of rock-smashing. It was, after all, her life's work, and she did her best to communicate the subtleties of her art. But Auntie Greta didn't have a way with words, exactly.

"First, we start with smacking it with our hands. When you are older, you will graduate to smashing it with a tool, but now you are young and must learn just to smack it."

Hannah nodded. "Yes, Auntie Greta."

"When you are done, you can go to bed."

Hannah made a feeble smack on the

rock, to show Auntie Greta that she would be good. Greta grunted in approval, which was all the goodnight Hannah would get, and shambled out of the room, her great bulk creaking the floorboards.

Such was Hannah's life at the Groebelfälters. She smacked half-heartedly at the rock, and her aunt and uncle Otto sat in the next room eating their evening sausages, not talking, just listening to make sure Hannah was doing her duty. Smack, chew, smack, swallow, smack, the clink of a fork.

Somehow, the sound of rock-smacking and lip-smacking formed itself into a feeble rhythm. It was no symphony, but for Hannah, who was constantly thinking about music, there was a certain beauty in it, and she could not help but make up a melody to go along with it. She began, very quietly, to hum.

"What's all that racket?" Aunt Greta loomed into the room.

"I was just humming a little tune, Auntie—"

"Music is forbidden here! No singing! Only rock-smacking!" squawked her aunt, her lumpy face red. Hannah could hear her uncle rustling angrily in the kitchen.

"But why, Auntie? Why can't I hum a little song?"

Greta bulged. "It is the way. We like peace and quiet here. Peace and quiet and rock-smashing."

"I don't want to smash rocks, Auntie Greta."

This flabbergasted Aunt Greta. Her fists wadded up into tight clumps, and her eyes protruded. "What on earth?" she stuttered. "What would you do with your life, then?"

Hannah meekly replied, "I would make music."

"Ludicrous! It is forbidden here!"

Hannah should have just taken that for an answer, as most children would have, but her life was so awful that she was filled with desperation. It overwhelmed her. She hated rocks. "Why is it forbidden?" she cried.

Greta reached a strange fit of anger, her fingers clenching and unclenching, her great coiled intestines twisting in her hard guts. Hannah recoiled—she had said something so evil it seemed to be causing her aunt a seizure. "Because it is very dangerous! Very, very dangerous! You don't know! You are too young to know!"

Suddenly, horribly, Aunt Greta's enormous shoulders began to heave. A single thick tear squeezed itself from between her muscled eyelids, and a mortal sob shook itself from within the cavernous depths of Auntie Greta's grey soul. Hannah watched in amazement and fear.

"What's going on in there?" came the stern voice of Uncle Otto. "Is that nasty little girl causing a ruckus? Shall I come in?" His hard boots hit the floor in the kitchen, his chair squeaked as he stood.

Greta called to her husband. "Nothing, dear husband. Just talking about rock-smashing." Then, to Hannah's surprise, her aunt leaned over very close and whispered in Hannah's ear.

"Go, go! If you must sing, go do it by

the river where nobody will hear you. Be careful, Hannah."

Hannah nodded in confusion. Greta clenched her arm meaningfully, staring her in the eye, as she called out again to her husband. "Well, that's a good girl, you're learning quickly. You will be a good rock-smasher some day. But now you must sleep. Good night."

And Hannah slipped out the window into the darkness.

Chapter Three

THE NIGHT AIR was chilly, but Hannah did not notice. She could not understand what had just happened, what bizarre secrets lead her aunt to behave in such a way, but she did not concern herself with it. All she knew was that, at the riverside, it was safe for her to sing.

Down the village streets she ran, past all the sleeping houses, all the old souls dreaming of rocks, past the moonlit quarry, and down to the riverbank.

Even the river did not burble musically, as poets sometimes like to say rivers do. It just burbled. But she found herself a rock to sit on, and, bursting with song, she looked around to make sure nobody was near.

The coast seemed clear, and she felt like a grand song of jubilation; her lungs were filled. But she knew to be careful. She had to preserve her new hiding place. If anybody caught her here, there would be nowhere else to go. So she summoned her restraint and sang softly.

It was a sad little tune when it came out. It was a song about happy warm places, where everybody loved to sing, where even the birds and the bears joined in, where the sun shone and everywhere

were grass and trees and flowers. It was a
sad song because she knew that this
happy place was never to be hers in reali-
ty, only in her imagination, sitting on a
cold rock next to a grey river in the dark.
But it was enough for poor Hannah,
enough for that night.

She thought nobody could hear her,
but she was wrong. But it was not an ordinary ear that listened. It was a tiny ear,
attached to a furry head. The furry head
had a whiskered face, and tiny eyes, filled
with a terrible loneliness. They stared
from beneath the sloshing surface of the
river, for the mysterious listener was
underwater.

It was an apparition that observed her.
His name was Oskar, and he was the ghost
of a rat. He had haunted that part of the

river for thirty desolate years, sorrowfully lurking in a cold crevice that was his cursed home, shivering, wet, silently weeping.

But tonight, unlike any other night in his unending watery vigil, a child had arrived, sat on a rock, and begun to sing. Oskar was filled with a joy he had not felt since he was alive. Half-remembered sunny days glimmered from inside his ghostly soul. He listened with a spectral tear in his little eye.

And finally, Hannah's song ended, and she got up to leave. Oskar couldn't stand to see her go. He summoned his strength, and emerged from the river.

"Wait!" he squeaked. Hannah stopped in her tracks, a chill wind on the back of her neck. She turned, and there, before

"Oh, once I was a rat," said Oskar, glumly.

her, shimmered a luminous rodent.

"By my soggy whiskers, child," he cried, "don't go! That was such a pretty song! How on earth did you get here?"

Hannah regarded the spectre before her. She stuttered. "I just moved here."

"Poor child! To live in this cursed place! You must be careful that they do not hear you singing."

"I know," said Hannah. "But pardon me, sir. Are you a rat?"

"Oh, once I was a rat," said Oskar, glumly. "Now I am nothing but the ghost of a rat, condemned to sit in this river for all eternity. Don't you know the story?"

"I'm new here," said Hannah.

"I thought everybody knew the story." Oskar grimaced at the memory. "I shall tell you what happened, then. It is a very sad tale." He touched his brow to summon his muse, and then struck a dramatic pose.

"Many years ago, Hamelin was a paradise for rats," he said. (Hamelin was the name of the town, as you might have guessed.) "The Hameliners made cheese, you see, and we lived fat and easy with all that cheese lying around. Oh, glorious cheese! The town was famous for it!" He paused for a moment, in respectful memory of cheeses past, and then continued.

"But the people were resentful, because they were selfish. They didn't want to share their delightful cheese, and they would chase us with brooms if they caught us munching. But in those days there were many, many of us rats, and the Hameliners were helpless to drive us out.

"But one day, a sinister man came to the village, who could play the flute like you wouldn't believe."

"A musician?" asked Hannah, eagerly.

"An evil musician. He was known as the Pied Piper. He claimed he could rid the town of rats. The greedy people of Hamelin offered him a great deal of gold to do it. And so he played his flute.

"What a song it was, Hannah. Like nothing we'd ever heard, a tune that went through our ears into our very hearts and made us all young again, made us old and wise, made us feel like we were full of cheese and yet also, somehow, like we were filled with an unutterable longing for a cheese that we would never taste. It took over our souls and drew us to follow him like he could lead us to our truest, innermost, forgotten home. Oh, that man could play the flute!

"But where did he lead us? With that enchanting music? We, poor, sensitive, stupid, romantic rats? To the river to drown."

"Oh no!" said Hannah. It was an awful tale. 'Those poor rats', she thought, but the worst was yet to come.

Oskar continued. "Not a single rat remained. Ever since then, Hamelin has been without joy."

"How awful. But why is there no music here?" asked Hannah.

Oskar leaned forward conspiratorially. "I'll tell you how it happened: When the Piper came to collect his fee, the town council thought to themselves: Well, the work is done, and after all, he's only a musician, what can he do to us? So they looked him in the eye and told him they wouldn't pay him."

"So what happened?" asked Hannah.

"The Piper was furious. He raged through the streets, shrieking and shaking his fists, but the townsfolk ignored  him. So he enacted a revenge upon them that has driven them mad. He played his flute a second time, and out of all the houses came the children. The parents wailed and gnashed their teeth, but the children were enchanted. They followed the Piper down the street and out into the mountains, to a secret place from which they have never returned.

"A cry of sorrow rose from the village on that day, and echoed through the cheese shops and cellars and cowstalls, until finally they had wept as much as can be wept. After that, silence. Music reminds them of their misdeeds. Well, it serves them right! We poor rats, all we ever wanted was a little cheese—"

It all became clear to Hannah. What a horrible place she had come to! What a cursed town! "Do you know what happened to the children?" she asked.

But Oskar had grown emotional. "How can anybody be happy without rats in the cellar? Without the delightful sound of us chewing away at their cheese? Without the pretty patter of our little feet in their walls? What lunacy possessed the people of Hamelin!"

"Yes, but what happened to the children?"

But the rat-ghost did not answer. "Look out!" he cried, and disappeared under the water.

Chapter Four

SUDDENLY, HANNAH'S STOMACH dropped: the crunch of a boot on rock, behind her. A grunt. A voice, gruff and terrifying.

"What is all that racket? Did I hear singing?"

Hannah tried to hide behind a rock, but too slow, oh, woe, too slow. For around the corner came Uncle Otto, a lantern swinging from his hand. He wore the tra-

Uncle Otto loomed.

ditional helmet of the town nightwatch, and his angry red eyes peered out from the shadows under the brim. His moustache was enormous and threatening, like a vicious animal attached to his face. From his waist there hung a scabbard, and in the scabbard was a very ugly sabre.

Uncle Otto loomed. Hannah shivered.

"You shame me," said Uncle Otto. "My own niece. The poison comes back to us, and it's my own flesh and blood that brings it." He bared his teeth, and clenched his lantern with a reddening fist.

"I'm sorry, Uncle Otto," said Hannah. "I'm ever so sorry. Please, give me another chance, and I'll be quiet and good." As she said it, her heart grew heavy, but she said it nonetheless. For what else could she say? "One more chance, please."

Uncle Otto stared at her, his moustache twitching. "No more chances," he said. He raised his hand to his mouth, and bellowed: "Music! Music! Alarm! Emergency! Music, by the River!"

Hannah covered her head with her arms, as the alarm traveled through the town like a screeching bullet. Windows flung open, fists were raised, throats shouted, boots stomped, torches were lit.

And soon, the entire village stood in a circle around Hannah. The riverside was bright now with the fire of their torches, and Hannah was surrounded by a horrible spinning crowd of beards and bulging eyes, necks straining with angry veins, shaking fists and furrowed brows.

"Singing, was she?"

"Wants to be the Pied Piper, does she?"

"Wants to cast a spell on us with her pretty little songs?"

The crowd began to howl and stomp in a deranged frenzy, like wolves or apes; it was a berserk primeval rage that shook them. Hannah could see nowhere to go, nowhere that wasn't blocked by an apoplectic Hameliner, barking and bellowing.

Out of the broiling crowd stepped the town mayor, an enormous man who had jowls like a toad and a towering hairstyle. As he stepped forward, the crowd hushed, awaiting his pronouncement.

He stood, his nightgown flapping about his pale legs, and glared down at poor whimpering Hannah. He addressed the crowd with a voice of rumbling authority.

"Look at her, Hameliners. She is, after all, just a child, is she not? Is she not young, and therefore ignorant? Can we blame her for it? For once, were we not also ignorant—ignorant of the evils of music? Surely we can see that. Surely we can see past our rage. Can we not see, dear Hameliners, that it would be unfair for us to hang this little girl? Would it not be unfair? The gallows are not for her, I say: the gallows must wait."

The villagers muttered amongst themselves, and shuffled. They had the whiff of blood in them, and they were not easily quelled.

"However!" said the mayor, his finger raised in the air. "However. She must learn, must she not? She must learn. And yet—how might she learn? How do we

"Is she not young, and therefore ignorant?"

deal with ignorance?"

He paused. "We teach. And so I say to you, little girl: You do not know what forces you have unleashed in this town. This town knows, more than any other town, the evils of music. Yes. For was it not in this town, so many years ago, that the Pied Piper came and stole our children? Without mercy! Without provocation! With what? With music!"

The crowd cheered, shaking their torches. "Curse the Pied Piper!" they bellowed. But the mayor raised his arms again, and they quieted down.

"Music is evil, little girl. Music is the source of all our sorrows. It cannot, under any circumstances, be allowed in this town. Never again. Do you understand me?"

"I understand," said Hannah, gratefully. "Never again."

"Good," said the Mayor. "Very good. And so, herewith I pass my judgement upon this girl, who says that she understands her crime. Are you ready for my judgement, good people of Hamelin?"

"Judgement! Judgement!" they cried.

"Exile," said the Mayor. "She must never set foot in this town again. She is a ghost to us."

Hannah gulped in fear. She looked from face to face in the torchlight. She looked up at the Mayor, past his belly, past his jowls, looking for a hint of sympathy. But he turned his head from her, and walked away. The crowd parted for his passing, and then, one by one, they turned their heads and walked away as well.

Last to turn away were Aunt Greta and

Uncle Otto. Aunt Greta looked sorrowfully at Hannah, but said nothing, as Otto put his arm around her shoulders and led her away.

And so, Hannah sat alone on her rock, abandoned. She was too shocked to cry.

Chapter Five

IN THE SHADOWS of the river, the ghost of the rat named Oskar watched with an expression of horror on his furry face. He looked sadly at poor Hannah, still sitting on her rock.

"I know how you feel," said Oskar. "They were none too fond of we rats, either."

"Yes, I imagine," said Hannah. But she couldn't really imagine. To be honest, she hadn't quite been able to absorb her current situation, let alone empathize with the plight of a spectral rodent. It seemed to her like she was in a strange bubble, and the rest of the world was muffled and slow and distant from inside of it. She stared blankly at her finger, which scratched her knee mechanically, as if it weren't a part of her at all, as if she had not willed it to do as it was doing, as if it were a curious appendage that had recently grown on her hand with which she was only just recently getting acquainted.

The river gurgled sympathetically. Oskar knitted his brow and wrung his little pink hands.

Slowly, Hannah came back to her senses. She blinked. She swallowed. She got up from the rock, and shook the sleep out of her leg. She looked around.

"I have absolutely no idea what to do or where to go," she said.

"I'm not entirely sure what to recommend," replied Oskar. "On the one hand: the town, where I don't think they want you. On the other: the mountains. Worse still."

"How can they be worse than that nasty town?" said Hannah, throwing her hands up in disgust.

"Why, they are the domain of the Pied Piper. Who knows what would happen to you out there? What if the Piper found you?"

"I don't know," cried Hannah. "What would the Piper do that the villagers haven't done? I can't just hide in the river like a drowned rat!" She didn't mean to say that.

"Goodness, little girl! Goodness me! The Pied Piper, child, is a murderous monster! He drowns rats for pleasure, and is responsible for the wholesale slaughter of my entire family, my entire tribe! But maybe you don't care about rats—you should still fear the Piper. For you are a child, are you not? He also hates children! He tortures them! He is merciless! He is evil! Beware the Pied Piper!"

"Where else can I go?" cried Hannah, who was getting to be a little bit hysterical. "If I'm to be tortured, then so be it!" (Not a little bit hysterical, actually. She was entirely flying off the handle.) "I don't know what else to do!"

And with that, she ran.

"Wait!" cried Oskar, but she did not hear.

CHAPTER FIVE

"Oh, no," he said to himself. He wrung his little hands. Another victim of the Piper! He had to do something. So he ran after her.

It was a place of fog and crag that she stumbled through.

Chapter Six

HANNAH FLED INTO the enormous night. Her pounding feet took her, leaping from rock to rock, the moon flickering through the tree branches as she sped to she-knew-not-where.

She followed the river's grey slosh and burble, careening along its banks as it wound its way into the hills. Mountains loomed around her, like slumbering frost giants; a cold wet wind blew amongst the rocks, making a grim rattle and moan. It was a place of fog and crag that she stumbled through, a place of shadow and scree. But where else could she have gone? With the town closed to her, she could only go deeper into that hard world of crevices and peaks.

Through the night she staggered on, blindly. But finally, her little lungs could breathe no longer, and her little feet couldn't hold her up. She sank first to her knees, and then to the ground, and then lay her head down to sleep.

She dreamt of music, there, bedraggled and cold on the frost-rimed ground, her knees bruised and dirty, pulled up to her chest, shivering. Music was her solace and her sanctuary. It was the one piece of good fortune granted to poor little

Hannah—that when life was dire, as it often was, she could always go inside her head and dream of music.

But it was not a dream of music that woke her. It was real. Real notes, real instruments, a real symphony playing nearby. At first she thought she was still asleep, the music was so beautiful. She thought she was still in her parents' house, warm under her covers, but slowly she felt the rock she was lying on and knew it wasn't her bed at all. She was still in the mountains, and there before her rose a mountain taller than all the others.

Its peak disappeared into the clouds, and its face was a stern cliff. The river ran right into it, through a dark tunnel, disappearing into its rocky depths. From within that river-cave came the music, sweet and full of longing, and it was like the music that Hannah heard in her head.

She stood for a moment savouring it in the morning sun. What glorious place could this be? How could there be a symphony out here? Had she slipped into dementia?

She picked her way down to the river, and stepped carefully from rock to rock along the bank and into the cave. With every step the music grew louder, even as the darkness closed over her, and the sun shone no longer on her passage.

Chapter Seven

ENORMITY OPENED BEFORE her. It was just like in her imagination: only much bigger. The ceiling arched out of sight, and the walls were distant crags. The river became a waterfall, tumbling down a cliff into a great dark lake, from which towered spires of wet rock, on the top of which sat huge lanterns casting a flickering firelight on the gently rippling water below.

There, in the centre of the cavern, was an island, and on the island was an orchestra. Hannah looked down at it with joy in her heart. The beautiful music came from there, that music that was like the sighs of angels to Hannah.

The orchestra moved like a many-limbed thing, breathing in unison to the music, swaying with each crescendo as if they had merged into one fabulous creature made of rosewood and brass, string and ivory, wind and horsehair. It was a strange assembly of men and women, dressed in tattered tails and dirty collars, their faces grimy and their hair askew in a fabulous composition like an aviary. But they played their instruments with incredible concentration. All among them had their eyes closed, their ears

twitching and straining with their determination to hear every note perfectly.
Their fingers flew across fret-boards and
clarinet keys; trumpets sang like tropical
birds; cellos moaned with an impossible
tragic joy; tympanies rumbled like thunder; violins wept to the heavens. Hannah
was overtaken by it; she could barely
stand on the edge of the cliff. Her knees
swayed.

And there, prancing before the
orchestra, was the wild-maned conductor.
He directed the orchestra with an intensi-
ty that was half-terrifying. His arms swept
through the air, slicing the baton like a
sabre, his hair barely able to hang onto his
thrashing head, his ragged coat tails
swishing like the wind. He pirouetted on
a trill, then pounced, stabbing at the bass

Prancing before the orchestra was the wild-maned conductor.

cello section, urging vigour, frothing with it; then in a single leap hurtling through the air to land before the oboes, wagging his fingers at them frantically, demonstrating notes, staring intently into their ears as if it would help them hear. With a high-pitched shriek, he spun in mid-air to summon the drums with his left foot and to spur staccato from the pianist with his right hand; while still suspended in his frenzied leap he nodded approval to the lead violinist and landed in exasperation before one poor clarinetist.

"Terrible! Terrible! Terrible! The Heavens are crumbling, because of you. The Gods are weeping! I can hear them from here, tearing at their hair! A total catastrophe! You, Ludwig, stand up!" the conductor cried, pointing his quavering baton at the clarinetist, who stood up slowly, his face long.

"You, I single you out. Ludwig, you are the very source of cosmic evil itself. You play like you are a soulless thing, an empty husk, devoid of feeling or even of brains."

Ludwig (for that was his name) gulped. He was rumpled even for this ramshackle company; his tie was crooked, and his jacket stained with gravy. But he had a kind face, worried, sincere.

"I'm sorry, Maestro," he said.

"I know you are sorry, Ludwig. It's a good sign that you feel regret. But the Gods are not so forgiving. They gnash their teeth at you, Ludwig. They wail and moan. Please, I beg you, in the name of the crystal spheres of heaven, in the name of vibrating strings and all that makes melodies, please, Ludwig—I'm on my knees—please go jump into the river. It'll be better that way. Show us you're sorry."

Ludwig held back a sob. "Yes, Maestro," he said.

"Good. Thank you. The whole world thanks you. Goodbye, Ludwig."

"Goodbye, Maestro." Ludwig put down his clarinet softly, lovingly; he gave it a forlorn stroke of farewell, and wiped a tear from his cheek. The conductor stood with his arms crossed as Ludwig gave a little wave to the rest of the orchestra, who regarded him with a certain distaste mingled with secret sympathy. He walked slowly away from the island.

"Well, now that that's all dealt with," the conductor said, as Ludwig trudged off, "we shall have to break for lunch. To the dining-room, children!"

And with that, the orchestra stood, bowed to the conductor, and the whole contraption of strings and fingers and ears and feet marched off the island and disappeared into a door on the far side of the cavern. The conductor himself headed off through a different door, grumbling about the day's proceedings.

Hannah sat dumbfounded. Such beautiful music, but such cruelty! That poor clarinetist.

Chapter Eight

THAT VERY SAME clarinetist suddenly appeared just a few feet from Hannah. His face was very distressed, with tear-stained cheeks. He had just climbed from below, and he heaved a great sad sigh as he clambered to the top of the cliff upon which Hannah was sitting. He had not seen Hannah; he turned to face the edge.

"Goodbye, world. It'll be better this

way," he said to the open air in front of him. "Weep not for poor Ludwig. He deserves his fate."

"Stop!" cried Hannah.

Ludwig almost fell off the cliff, he was so shocked. "Eurgh," he stammered. "Who are you?"

"I'm Hannah," replied Hannah, feeling rather a lot like it wasn't quite the most important thing to be discussing. "Don't jump!" she told him. "It wasn't that bad!"

Ludwig shook his head. "Oh, yes, it was. The Maestro said so."

"But you'll get better," said Hannah. It seemed true.

"I'll never get any better," Ludwig said, sadly, and braced himself for his mortal jump. "Goodbye."

"Stop!" cried Hannah, and grabbed

"Weep not for poor Ludwig. He deserves his fate."

Ludwig around the waist.

Ludwig struggled to free himself. "Listen, I've got jumping in the river to do," he cried. "What do you want?"

"I've come to play music," she said. As it came out of her mouth, she realized that it was indeed true. Perhaps her exile was a great thing after all. A life in an orchestra! It was a shimmering, glorious idea. What if it could come true?

Ludwig paused, a glimmer of fanaticism in his eyes. "Well, you've come to the right place," he said. "That's all we do here. The Maestro is the greatest music teacher that ever was."

"He's very strict," pointed out Hannah.

"He must be. We need his guidance to be rigid, or we will never learn. We are very happy here. You should join us. Or, rather, them, for I must jump into the river now."

"No, you don't," said Hannah. "You don't have to jump in the river just because he said so! Why are you being so ridiculous?"

"Because I am enchanted! I must do as he says!" cried Ludwig. His face crumpled as he said it, and he began to sniffle. His eyes brimmed with tears. "I miss my Mum and Dad," he sobbed. "I want to go home."

Hannah regarded him in amazement. It was strange and terrible to see a grown man cry like that, but what on earth was he saying? "Shh, it's okay," said Hannah, taking him by the shoulder, which shook gently with his emotion. "It'll be okay." But it was only now becoming clear to

Hannah what exactly she had stumbled upon.

Ludwig twitched and pulled himself free of Hannah. He looked at her bravely through his tears. "Listen, it's been nice talking to you," he said, "but I must go jump in the river now, or the Maestro will be very angry with me." With that, he stepped to the brink.

"Please, don't do it!" cried Hannah, as the man extended his foot out over the edge, closed his eyes, and drew a shuddering breath.

"Goodbye," he said.

Chapter Nine

GOOD MORNING, CHILDREN! Time for rehearsal! Ludwig, come down from there! Where am I going to get another clarinetist? Quit futzing around on that cliff!" The conductor stormed back onto the island, and the orchestra poured out of their door, clamouring back to their seats.

Ludwig breathed a sigh of relief and put his foot back down on the ground.

"I have to go," he said to Hannah, and began his climb back down.

"Back to him? He just asked you to jump in the river!"

"I must do as he says. I told you—I am enchanted."

The mad conductor's voice came from below, furious at waiting. "Ludwig! What on earth are you doing?"

"Sorry, Maestro, I'm coming."

There was a shocked pause from below. The conductor's voice came in a strangled cry. "Who is that?"

Ludwig looked at Hannah in horror, frozen to the cliff. Hannah did not know what to do. She did the only thing she could think of: She answered.

"My name's Hannah."

The conductor stood, peering into the

"Ludwig! Bring that girl down here this instant!"

darkness at the little girl who had so astonishingly appeared in his cavern.

"Hannah," he repeated.

'Yes. I'm here to learn about music."

"You are, are you?" The conductor ruminated for a moment. Ludwig gulped. Hannah tried not to breathe.

"Ludwig! Bring that little girl down here this instant!"

Ludwig nodded enthusiastically and extended his hand to Hannah, who, quaking, took it. Together they clambered down the cliff, and Ludwig led her across the bridge to stand in front of the Maestro himself. Ludwig scampered back to his seat and clasped his clarinet to his chest. The whole orchestra watched in confusion and excitement.

The conductor was much taller than

he had appeared from above. He had the appearance of a huge and ancient tree: his hands were crooked and dry like dead branches, his eyebrows were shaggy and wild like unruly moss, his face gnarled like knotted bark. His nostrils flared.

"Well, you've come to the right place, then. Welcome to the Pied Piper's School of Music for Children. You may call me Maestro."

"Desire is nothing. Excellence is what is required."

Chapter Ten

THE PIPER STOOD looming over Hannah, who quailed now with fear. Here he stood: murderer of rats, stealer of children, destroyer of joy in Hamelin. He was more terrifying than she had imagined—more coiled, more severe, and far more imperious. She had pictured a devilishly handsome fellow, debonair and worldly; evil, yes, but was he not also a musician? But this man was all crag and furrow.

He stared down at her and bellowed. "What can you play?"

Hannah looked up at him, her hands folded in the way that she had been taught was polite, fear in her belly. Her knees shook and she hoped it wasn't noticeable.

"I can sing," she offered.

The Piper pointed at the orchestra. "This is an orchestra," he said. "Singing is not required. You can't play any instruments?"

Hannah looked at the orchestra, who sat tensely, watching the events unfold. She wanted with all her heart to be amongst them, to be a musician like them, to spend her life in that glorious company. But she couldn't play any instruments; she had only been taught how to smash rocks, after all, and she didn't think that counted.

"Well, not yet," she said.

The Piper frowned. "You are profoundly behind. All these children can play instruments, with the possible exception of Ludwig, of course." He turned and glowered at Ludwig, who nodded apologetically. The Piper turned back to Hannah. "I'm afraid we don't have much use for you."

Hannah felt her knees about to give out entirely. To be chased from the town was one thing, horrible enough—but this was an orchestra. All that stood between her and that great happiness was this evil Pied Piper, who glowered at her like the Angel of Death at heaven's gate, both terrible and mighty.

"But it's all I want to do!" she cried, and felt hot tears coming to her eyes.

The Piper huffed impatiently. "Desire is nothing. Excellence is what is required. And that through discipline. Through practice. Through invincible will. It must be paid for."

He stared at Hannah with fire instead of eyes. "This is Music we are making. It is not some toy you see in a window, to make you cry 'I want' and smudge the glass with your runny nose and your greedy eyes. This is Art, child. You may want it. But that is irrelevant. The question is: Does Art want you?"

Hannah held her tears, and stared back at the Maestro with as much determination as she could muster.

"Well," he said. 'We shall see. Play this."

He grabbed Ludwig's clarinet, and extended it to Hannah, his eyes piercing. "There might just be an opening for a clarinetist of sufficient talent."

Hannah looked at Ludwig, who was mortified, but who still (kind soul that he was) tried to demonstrate a fingering position in the air, as if that could help. He did his best. Hannah bravely put the thing to her lips, checked to see if her fingers were doing anything like what Ludwig was showing her, drew a breath, and blew.

What came out was the most wretched squeak she had ever heard. It was the squeak of a drowning rat, the squeak of "music is forbidden here," the squeak of unutterable failure. Hannah lost all her nerve in that bottomless moment.

"Stop! Hopeless! I can't bear it!" cried the Maestro, covering his ears, grimacing. Hannah stopped.

Silence. Meekly, she spoke. "Give me a moment, I'll figure it out."

But the Piper snorted. "I do not have the patience," he said. "We have too much to do, and too little time. Please, the river is over there." He handed the clarinet back to Ludwig, and pointed the way for Hannah.

Hannah began (and who can blame her? Certainly not I) to cry. She just stood there; she couldn't move her legs, she couldn't seem to breathe. The Piper was exasperated.

Hannah looked up at him, saw him fuming, and, bless her plucky little heart, she became angry. "I'm not going to jump in any river," she cried. "I'm here to play music, not to be bossed around by some nasty man! There's nowhere else I can go, now that I've been banished from that stupid town for singing."

"Banished for singing?" said the Piper, arching his eyebrows. "Is it Hamelin you are talking about, little girl? That hideous, deranged, ungrateful little town?"

Hannah was so full of frustration, so brimming with rage, that she could no longer tell who she was angry at.

"It's not a hideous little town," she cried. "Once it was a happy place, full of children, until you came and stole them all away!" Hannah was surprised at her bravery; she swelled with it. She turned to the musicians, and raised her little fist in the air defiantly. "Rise up, orchestra, you don't have to live this way! Revolt against this cruel man!" she cried. "Go back to your mothers and fathers!"

The Piper frowned. The orchestra quavered. "Enough of you," he said, menacingly. He turned away from her, and raised his baton. "Orchestra! Instruments up! Play!" he cried, and the orchestra obeyed.

And suddenly Hannah felt herself running, staggering, splashing through the water, blinded by tears, throwing open doors, her feet pounding down hallways, the beautiful sounds of the orchestra growing more and more muffled as she ran.

Chapter Eleven

S HE AWOKE IN a closet much like the one in her aunt and uncle's house. She must have found it in her delirium, and hidden in it. She could see out through the crack of the door, which let in enough light to show her she was surrounded by musty coats and sweaters hanging in disarray. She crumpled up in a ball amongst some old shoes and pondered her situation.

There was absolutely nothing good about it. Exiled from a town she hated anyway, kept from the life of her dreams by the cruelty of that horrible man. It was terrible to think that the world had no music in it at all, but even worse to know that this orchestra existed without her. The whole universe was bleak without end. Perhaps there was nothing for it but the river after all.

But she heard something. A door creak, a footstep. She mustered the strength to peek out of the closet.

She was in somebody's bedroom. There was a decrepit four-posted bed, stained carpets, dark wooded furniture, and a dusty lamp. Underneath the grime, everything had once been very fine, but it was all now well beyond repair. Even the air was thick with age.

She jumped in her skin. The Pied Piper was there, sitting in a chair, his grizzled head in his hands. He was murmuring to himself madly.

"Stolen! I didn't steal the children. I saved them! They were being raised by monsters. Vile, vile, village, that hears the most beautiful music in the world and then won't pay for it! They can keep their foul gold, and their ignorance. They were beyond redemption. But the children had a chance. I could not see them be wasted in such a purgatory!"

He lifted his head, and spoke strangely, imploring the wall as if it were the orchestra.

"Music—children, you must understand—music is a spell. It is mysterious; it

He was murmuring to himself madly.

is not just notes on a page, something vibrating in your ear: it is an enchantment. When you are in the presence of music, you are not yourself. You are another, better person. Listen! I have brought you here to teach you the secrets of the cosmos, to make you into sorcerers. Forget your drudgerous homes and your ignorant mothers and fathers: an artist has no home but Art. Do not shirk your duty!"

He leaned back in his chair, a lunatic glaze in his eyes. His hands fluttered up, and she realized he was conducting into thin air. Little hums and grunts escaped from his lips, and his eyelids fluttered. "Yes, that's it," he mumbled. "Perfect, children, good! Play, my little ones! Beautiful!"

Music unheard of by humankind was playing in his brain—music so fragile and perfect that only madness could conceive it. It was the music that the Pied Piper heard whenever he closed his eyes, whenever he tried to sleep, which he could never do: The symphony of the heavens would not let him rest. His body failed, his muscles slackened, his breath slowed, his hands fell, and the music coursed through his veins with an unbearable glory. The Maestro hung his head back and listened.

Many people might not have understood what was happening; they might have thought the Maestro was beyond sanity. But Hannah understood. She knew all too well the agony of perfect sounds in her head that would never become real. She wept for the Maestro, and for herself.

The two sat in their separate lonely places, the Piper totally unaware that he was being watched, and Hannah lost in her own sorrow.

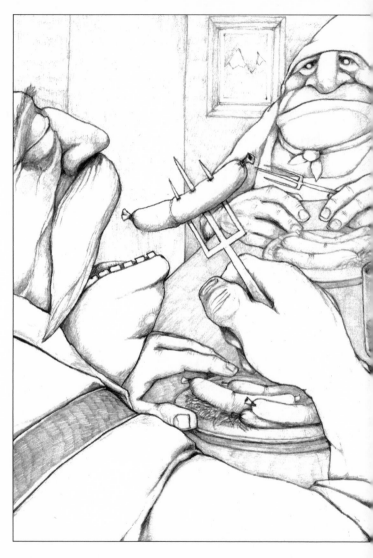

Meanwhile, Aunt Greta stared listlessly at her sausages.

Chapter Twelve

MEANWHILE, AUNT GRETA stared listlessly at her sausages. Across from her, her husband Otto's moustache went up and down with his chewing, his jaw mindlessly determined in its labours. His eyes were blank as he sliced another piece and raised it to his mouth.

Greta had no appetite. She had lost it on the night Hannah was exiled. In fact, she had not simply lost her appetite for sausages. She had lost a deeper appetite as well. She took too long to get out of bed in the morning, and longed to be back in it all day. She found no joy in sauerkraut. And she could not face her rock-pick.

All these years of digging! For this was why they tunneled: they searched for their children in the mountains. But every cavern they uncovered was dark and empty, and Greta had lost hope. The children were gone forever. And finally a child had come to them, but they had been blinded by their guilt, made lunatic by their sorrow. What had they done?

And now, Hannah was gone, probably frozen in a mountain pass somewhere, or— worse—in the clutches of the Piper. And, when it came right down to it, it was Greta herself who had told her to sing by the river. She had thought it would be safe, but how wrong she had been! Greta had unwittingly sent poor Hannah to her doom.

Otto belched and wiped his moustache with his napkin. He pushed his empty plate away from himself, grunted at Greta, and then tucked his chin to his chest for his after-dinner nap. His enormous eyelids closed with a dull thud and soon enough he was snoring in his chair.

Greta collected the dishes and shuffled into the kitchen. She stood at the sink for a moment, staring at the wall, and thought mournfully of Hannah. She trudged to Hannah's empty little bedroom, and stood feeling old and tired at the door. She sighed. The steady rumble and hoot of Otto's snoring in the background was the only sound.

"Madame," whispered a voice, suddenly,

and Greta's heart jumped within her enormous chest. She searched the shadows for the source of that voice, but could see nothing.

"If you will excuse me," continued the voice, "I believe we have a common objective: revenge upon the Pied Piper. And I believe we can accomplish it together. But in order for us to work together for this goal, it is extremely important that you do not make a fuss right now. You must listen to what I have to say before making any rash decisions. Will you agree to this?"

Greta furrowed her brow, and peered into the shadows. She could not see a thing. "I will agree," she said, slowly.

"Good," said the voice. And Oskar, the ghost of a rat, appeared before her.

"I followed Hannah into the mountains," he said. "I know where your children are."

Chapter Thirteen

Finally, the Piper rose unsteadily to his feet. Hannah regarded him quietly from inside the closet, and watched as he went to his dresser and opened the bottom drawer. His back creaked as he stood, having retrieved a long wooden box, which he placed on his bed and carefully opened.

Inside was a silver flute. With shaking hands he lifted it from its velvet bed and stroked it gently, putting it briefly to his lips and then looking at it again. "Ah, me," he sighed. "I am so very old. My fingers will no longer play you, my lovely one. But what music we once made!"

His eyes glazed for a moment, as his youth glimmered in his mind: him, strong, tall, handsome, his coat a brilliant azure, his eyes dark and brooding in a way that women found irresistible. And possessed! He was fire and wine, he was a sob and a cry, when he played that flute. He swept from town to town like a frenzied wind, breaking hearts and then off again in the sunny, misty mornings to come like a hurricane into some new valley or to blow over some new prairie, his flute snorting flames like a glittering and deadly dragon in the sky. Oh, he was a grand one, indeed.

Oh, he was a grand one, indeed.

But soon, it would all be forgotten. For soon, he would pass from this earth, and all the secrets of his trade would pass with him. All the arcane ornamentations, the mystic arpeggios, the occult variations, all would seep into the silent earth along with him.

He couldn't bear the thought. His ancient hands quaked as he put the flute back in its case, and fondly closed the lid. His breathing was laboured, and his back hunched. Hannah realized now just how terribly old he really was.

He stared at the box. "What use are you, if you don't last forever?" he said, sadly.

Suddenly, he raised his grey head, and shouted: "Children! Children! Rehearsal time!" And with that, he stumbled from the room.

Hannah waited for a little while before she was brave enough to come out of her closet. She went to the door of the room, and listened at it, to make sure that nobody was on the other side.

In the distance, she heard the tramp of many feet, and the voice of the Piper calling instructions. "Dinner time is over now, children. To the rehearsal hall. No more chatter!"

Carefully, she pushed the door open. A draught of fresh air blew in, and the sounds of the orchestra going to practice became clearer.

Hannah kept to the shadows like some kind of cave-goblin, sneaking from crevice to crevice, padding quietly in the darkness. Her plan was not well formed, but it was the best she could come up with: She would hide, and listen.

Through great dusty galleries she snuck, and long twisting staircases. Through draughty corridors, creaking doors, attics and cellars. Echoes followed her through the deserted crannies, but she listened as she crept and finally she emerged from a narrow passage and came to the concert hall.

Her best vantage point seemed to still be the rock where she had first entered the mountain, so she crept there. She was enormously happy to find that someone had left her a bit of food, and ate it quietly, crouched, listening to the orchestra tune.

And then, Hannah watched as the Piper took his place at the podium, frail, held upward only by a will like cruel steel. But it was horribly evident that his mortality was close upon him.

He raised a quivering baton, and addressed the orchestra. "Children: It is rehearsal time," he said. "No ordinary rehearsal time. Today we will play music to the heavens; today the Gods will weep for joy; today the cosmos itself will swell with the majesty of our art. Eternity awaits us. Now, play, my little ones. Play!"

And the orchestra played. As the music surged, so too did strength surge back into the Maestro; his back straightened, his eyes flashed again, his arms raised in supplication.

"Yes, yes!" he cried. "The gates of heaven swing open! The angels welcome us with platters of olives and cheese! They show us down the glittering halls to our happy beds! We shall live forever, children! We shall never rot!"

"Oh, Art!" he moaned. "Thou art no cure for mortality."

He sprung from foot to foot, then leapt into the air, arms thrashing with each crashing note. His face gleamed with the light of heaven. "Good! Yes! Clarinet!"

He landed nimbly on his feet, and thrust his face to inches away from poor Ludwig, who knew his moment, but was filled with such trepidation and terror that his one note came out a sad little poot. The entire orchestra ground to a horrified halt. The Maestro staggered backwards as if hit by a cannonball. His voice, when he found it, was choked with despair.

"Oh, Art!" he moaned. "Thou art no cure for our mortality. Thou only seemest to be: But in truth it is thee who makes us fear it, by showing us hope."

He fell forward onto Ludwig, and

grabbed him by the collar, his mad eyes locked into Ludwig's. "Ludwig! Ludwig! Catastrophe!"

Ludwig held back his tears. "Sorry, Maestro."

The Piper stood slowly, and straightened his coat. He breathed with the calm of the doomed, and spoke softly. "You know what to do. I will retire to my chambers to cover my head with the rug and wail with sorrow because of you. Goodbye, children."

The Maestro walked across the bridge and into his door. The orchestra sat quietly. Ludwig put his clarinet down and felt sure that this time the Maestro would not stop him. He could see that the Maestro was too weak.

Chapter Fourteen

THE FOREST: PEACEFUL, quiet. The leaves rustling, the river burbling.

A low thrum in the distance, that slowly becomes a screeching and chattering, and scampering, swishing, rustling. And then, through the trees, comes a dark horde of rats.

They are like a dank breath of wind blowing through the forest, that phantasmal throng. They race, they swarm,

They murderously tromp.

towards the cave of the Piper. At their head skitters Oskar, leading the charge.

Then: the tramp of boots, the crush of grass, the smell of sweat. Following the rats, grim-faced, determined, the town guard. Their moustaches implacable. Their muskets like an iron fence, on their shoulders, bayoneted with long cruel knives. Their black helmets glint.

They march towards the cave as well. At their head, carrying a crimson banner, Greta. And behind her, Otto. They murderously tromp.

Chapter Fifteen

Not you again!" cried Ludwig, as Hannah leapt from the shadows to grab him before he jumped.

"Shhh!" said Hannah, covering his mouth with her hand. Ludwig struggled a little, but Hannah's will was too strong, and Ludwig's too weak. He nodded agreement.

Hannah released him. She beckoned urgently for him to follow, and, as soon as she could see that he understood, she scampered off into the darkness. Ludwig plodded after her.

Once they were safely out of earshot, Hannah stopped in the darkness, and whispered again into Ludwig's ear.

"Do you remember the song the Piper played on that day, Ludwig?"

"Of course I remember it," said Ludwig. "It's all I can ever think about. It was so beautiful, Hannah. All I've ever wanted to do since I heard it was to be able to play it. I dream of it, every night, but in the morning I just can't seem to get the notes right."

A plan burned within Hannah. It was a dangerous plan, but Hannah was in a desperate situation. "Could you teach it to me?" she whispered.

"I could," said Ludwig. "I could tell you kind of how it goes, anyway."

"That'll have to do," said Hannah, her brow determined. "Let's go, then."

They took each other by the hand, so they wouldn't lose each other in the dark. Together they went to a place deep in the mountain, and Ludwig taught Hannah the most beautiful melody in the entire world.

Chapter Sixteen

A HARROWING SHRIEK ECHOED through the caverns of the Pied Piper's School of Music for Children. The orchestra cringed, their skin prickling. They murmured amongst themselves nervously, sitting with their instruments in the concert hall, unsure of what to do.

Another shriek. "Leave me alone! I repent! I repent! Go away!" It was the hoarse shout of the Maestro, strange with fright.

Suddenly, then, the Maestro burst into the room, howling, hysterical, pursued by hundreds of spectral rats. He ran, hurtling from precipice to precipice, desperately aiming for higher ground. But the ghosts swirled and whirled about him in a maelstrom of screeching; he thrashed his arms about his head as he ran, shouting: "Please! Mercy! Blame the town! I am innocent!"

"Sleep no more!" cried the rats, as the Maestro stumbled and fell, groaning, swatting, whimpering.

The orchestra scrambled to escape, clutching their instruments to their bodies, their coat tails flapping like panicking crows in a flurry. They crashed into each other in their desperation, their flight muddled by confusion.

Then, from the cliff, a volley of shots resounded. Sizzling bullets screamed through the air, striking rocks in a hail of sparks and spinning in twisting hot arcs to land with a hiss in the water. The Maestro, covered in dust, cowered and wondered if he had been hit. He thought perhaps he had not.

All turned to see, and there stood the town guard, plumed by gunsmoke, resplendent and implacable in their steel helmets. Otto Groebelfälter stood with his sabre raised, his moustache erect. "Reload!" he cried; and the guard set to their task.

The Maestro staggered to his feet and ran again, his eyes glowing now with hatred, his face fierce. "I curse you!" he bellowed, hurling himself towards a near-

"I curse you!" he bellowed.

by door. "You don't know what you are destroying!"

But he was too far from the door; he was too slow, or the guardsmen too fast. "Aim!" cried Otto, and the thicket of musket barrels swung to their lines with a hollow rattle. The Maestro was leaping now, through the air; Otto's sabre flashed, the fingers squeezed their triggers, the bullets twitched, the powder itched.

"Stop!" cried Hannah.

Everything hung suspended. And then, Hannah began to sing.

The orchestra stood in confusion, this little girl before them, singing as if her life depended on it. I cannot describe to you what that song was like: It was a song that could only be sung if your life depended on it, if you wanted it that much. It was a song that made adults remember their unblemished childhoods, made time disappear, made the angels stop singing their eternal song so they could listen. It was holy and it was all the earth, it was lightning and thunder and peace and war and the last words of the old and the first cry of the newborn. Nothing like it could have come from Hannah's lungs if it were not at such a moment. Perhaps you can imagine music like it, or perhaps some day you, too, will hear it, but it cannot be described.

Hannah sang, and behind her rose the haggard figure of the Maestro. He took his place at the podium, and nodded to the orchestra, and as Hannah heaved her lungs to reach the high note, the orchestra raised their instruments and joined in.

CHAPTER SIXTEEN

The Maestro towered before them, blazing like an angelic revelation, his baton twirling and his hands fluttering. The orchestra soared with it, their fingers and lips did things they had never done before. The music reached the glowing embers of God's heart, and then floated back to glorious earth and then, silence.

The Town Guard stood with their moustaches drooping. Otto and Greta looked at each other with tears in their eyes. They had not heard music for thirty years. They could not speak.

The spectral rat horde sat perfectly still, sniffling, moved. Their tiny eyes glistened as well. Oskar blew his nose.

The orchestra sat, dazed and dwarfed by the enormity of what had just come out of themselves.

Ludwig stared in amazement at his clarinet, which had never before made such music, and at his fingers which had never before moved the way they were supposed to.

The Pied Piper himself had a broad grin on his face. "That was really quite good," he said. "Quite good, indeed. Ludwig, well done. Little girl, well done." He swayed a little, but managed to keep his balance.

"I'd like to go home," said Ludwig, quietly. "I miss my Mum and Dad."

The orchestra murmured in agreement. The Maestro hung his head. "Yes, Ludwig, you must go home."

"We're all going home," Ludwig said. "All of us."

The Piper looked at all of them, the

orchestra sitting there, exhausted, middle-aged, dirty.

"You may all go home now," he said.

The Maestro dropped his baton, and stood silently as the orchestra put down their instruments and slowly stood. They looked at each other blinking, and began to shuffle from the stage.

Hannah spoke. "If it's all right, I'd like to stay."

"Stay?" the Piper stared at her.

"All I want to do is play music. I could be your student."

"Yes," said the Piper. "I would like that."

Joy returned to the village.

Chapter Seventeen

THEY MADE A glorious parade, marching back to Hamelin, and with the parade, joy returned to the village as well.

Rock-picks and shovels rusted in the musty corners of basements, as the town returned to cheese-making, and soon happy tables buckled under the weight of glorious cheese platters.

Cheese, it turned out, was Ludwig's passion, and soon he was the chief cheesemaker in the village. He would hum beautifully to himself as he worked at the great curd-vats.

His mother and father, Greta and Otto Groebelfälter, were very proud of him, both because he was very good at what he did and also because his humming made the work a little more pleasant for everybody.

And the rats were welcomed back into the village. There was plenty to eat for everybody (and, after all, ghosts don't actually eat). All was forgiven. Oskar and Greta struck up a pleasant friendship and had tea every Wednesday.

Hannah and the Pied Piper still lived in the mountain, and gave wonderful concerts for all the people of Hamelin every Saturday afternoon. Hamelin became famous for its orchestra. Eventually, it became known as Maestro Hannah's Orchestra Under the Mountain.

And that's the end of the story.

THE MAESTRO is also a play called THE MYS-
TERIOUS MAESTRO that is performed with
symphony orchestras all over North America. It is
produced by DANDI productions; the story and
script were by Judd Palmer, and the puppets by The
Old Trout Puppet Workshop. The costumes were
done by Tara Kozak, and the original music and
orchestrations were by Dave Pierce and Donovan
Seidle. It was commissioned and adapted for
orchestra by DANDI Productions.

At its premiere on November 3rd, 2001, it was
performed by Doug McKeag, Onalea Gilbertson
and Dave Clarke, with the Edmonton Symphony
Orchestra.

G · O · O · D ·

THE
END

· N · I · G · H · T ·